NOD'S WAY

the Author's Edition

by

Robert Stikmanz

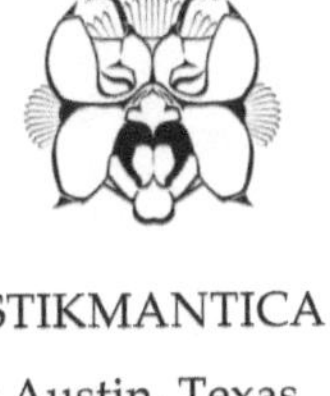

STIKMANTICA

Austin, Texas

Nod's Way, the Author's Edition © 2019 & 2021 by Robert D. Lewis
Cover art, book design & entire contents by Robert Stikmanz
0811021

ISBN: 978-1-7321187-3-7

Cataloging Data
Nod's Way, the Author's Edition / Robert Stikmanz
        p. 112   cm.
        ISBN: 978-1-7321187-2-0
        I. Stikmanz, Robert
                1. Fantasy – Divination
                2. Invented languages in literature
                3. Fictive art
        II. Title

STIKMANTICA
stikmantica.com

Acknowledgments

Patronage support for Stikmantica and this project came from Jim Eidson, Jill Fang, Thomas Fang, Charles M. Gatlin, Jr., Glenn Lewis, Mark Lewis, Bill Luthans, Bram Meehan, Nancy Salay, and Erin Severe-Fudge.

Rick Adams, Paul E. Cooley, Carol Daeley, Kenneth Kidder, James Rossignol, Randi Bunch Schultz, Kim Beauchemin Scoulios, and Tom Wheeler gave generously to breathe life into the work.

Thomas Fang's feedback on a late proof helped guide final preparation of this book.

Mopestar Media's Martin McCreadie has answered every plea to keep the Stikmantica web presence able.

I am grateful to all of them.

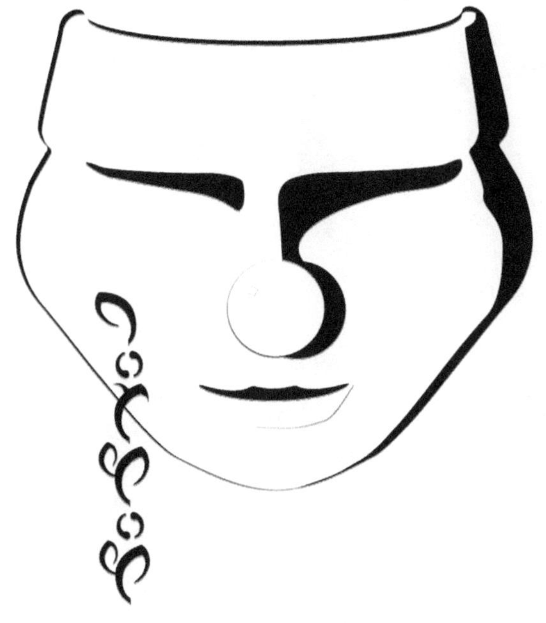

Nod's Way

Table of Contents

Introduction

Nod's Way, also known as *Hidden Dragon*, sprang alongside Dvarsh civilization from the age of legends. Its basic plan and earliest parts were set down more than eighteen thousand years ago by a figure so mysterious that the least controversial identification is, "a clown-like manifestation of unexpected personality." Subsequent additions to the core text have been bound with it for millennia, and yet, as oracle and lore its partisans find it constantly fresh. Education among the Dvarsh starts with learning to read and write by copying *Nod's Way*. From childhood, students embrace it more as a friend than a relic. At once a treasured tie to the deep past, the poetic statement of a living ethic, and an instrument for play, the book embodies the wisdom of a hidden people.

Nod, the Source

That "clown-like manifestation of unexpected personality" after whom the book is called, Nod[1] chose the symbols, organized their pairs, named them, wrote a brief declaration known as "the image" for each, and introduced the two matched dice called *The Companions*. No one disputes this. Also agreed is that these Nod-sourced elements survive intact from the earliest version, albeit translated into modern Dvarsh.

Nothing else can be pinned with certainty. Loose consensus points to a span of roughly seven hundred years during which the visitor is believed usually to have been present somewhere among the Dvarsh. Surviving comment from those personally acquainted with Nod uniformly recall a mask-like face with a shiny red nose.

After seven centuries, a day dawned on a world from which the unexpected personality had departed. Left behind, like a love song on time-release, was a way called *Hidden Dragon*.

Emo Azek

Second only to Nod as a spawner of culture, Emo Azek is just as enigmatic. A mage of the *dvarsh zek*, she is credited with discovering zero. It is uniformly agreed she lived a long time ago, although no one is sure exactly when. Some stories make her contemporary with Nod, others a predecessor, and others an heir. It is generally held that she had two daughters. Beyond that, not even shreds of legends about her name and lineage are remembered. The cognomen, Emo Azek, is an irregular form suggesting both "Zek person zero" and "Zero of [the] Zek." Perhaps because facts are scant, tales abound.

---

[1] See discussion of Nod in *Dvarsh, An Introduction*.

Estimates of her impact on *Nod's Way* vary according to how strictly a given authority traces the *Lenses* to teaching she inspired. Tradition attributes "Numeracy" and "Before Counting" to Emo Azek herself. There is a chance the first is so, but the second is not likely. Language in "Before Counting" seems consistent with relatively late authorship.

Nod's Way and *Hidden Dragon*

With its appeal to chance, the oracle was at first a teaching aid for an ethic Nod called *Hidden Dragon*. The term represents the un-tapped power of one's potential, as well as the eventual reward of oracular play. *Hidden Dragon* is preserved as a subtitle, but the book has been known familiarly as *Nod's Way* for millennia.

Content of the book

The oracle proper consists of thirty-six brief chapters, each associated with a pair of symbols. These chapters, or auspices, are grouped into three "houses" bound with an appendix of additional material.

The Moon House, *The Star House*, and *The Great Assembly* are defined by the types of symbols identified with the auspices they include. Four moon symbols and four star symbols pair in thirty-six combinations—ten moon with moon, ten star with star and sixteen moon with star. Each combination is assigned an auspice, which is named and placed according to its symbols in one of the houses.

The main body of each auspice is built around the elements that descend directly from Nod: its pair of symbols, its place in the order, its name and its image. The image is followed always by a comment on it, which in turn is followed usually but not always by a short declaration. Every auspice also includes references to calendar, resonance and compass, as well as remarks connected to "Ring" and "Bar."

In the past, the oracle was consulted using three special dice.[2] Two, called *The Companions*, were identical, eight-sided dice that bear the moon and star symbols on their faces. The third, called *The Odd Die*, was a cube blank except for emblems—a ring and a bar—on two diametrically opposite sides. *The Companions* determined the auspice of a cast. The cube came into play only if one of its marked faces showed topmost. In that case the "Ring" or "Bar" remark (whichever is indicated) was also part of the response.

The Great Boz'

Unlike the images, which are credited to Nod, the different comments, and certainly the declarations, have diverse origins. Casual use through centuries spun off countless interpretations.

---

[2] *Nod's Way* dice have passed into legend.

Those now accepted as received text were culled and edited by the Great Boz', a monastic dyad—what humans might call spouses—whose life work resulted in the modern form of the book.

Three elements of an auspice that follow the declaration—the references to calendar, resonance and compass—hark back to Emo Azek. The Ring and Bar remarks, however, derive from an older, coin-toss oracle that attached to *Nod's Way* in the remote past. The Great Boz' edited the present remarks from different takes on the coin-toss, and incorporated the result into the auspices. At that time they also introduced the innovation of *The Odd Die*.

Lenses

After the three houses, an appendix, called *Lenses*, includes ancillary documents selected by The Great Boz'. Two of these, a table of numeric values of the symbols and the Dvarsh calendar, are self-explanatory. Two others, "Numeracy" and "Before Counting," simply are what they are. The fifth lens, the compass, may be almost but not quite familiar.

The Dvarsh compass is organized around twelve directions instead of eight. Directions group in quarters of three centered on the cardinal points. Thus, the northern quarter centers on the direction, north, but includes also westnorth and eastnorth. Westnorth is the westerly direction of the northern quarter, as eastnorth is the easterly. Similarly, northeast is the northerly direction of the eastern quarter.

Referencing the compass diagram (see *Lenses*), counterclockwise of a point is its *falling* aspect, and clockwise is its *rising*.[3] Each point proper marks the "true" or "due" direction, which is called its *standing* aspect. All points together describe a total of thirty-six aspects of the compass. The thirty-six aspects of the compass map to the thirty-six auspices of the oracle.

The purpose of the compass and other *Lenses* is to stimulate interpretation.

---

[3] See explanation of "rising" and "falling" in *Dvarsh, an Introduction.*

How to consult the oracle

Among the Dvarsh, many know all of *Nod's Way* by heart. Some sprinkle it through their speech as though quoting scripture. Consulting the oracle can be solemn ritual or gaming play, but every approach encounters its advocacy for responsible life.

Typically, queries are made to clarify thought. A question or perplexity may be stated aloud, written on a scrap of paper, noted in a journal, or otherwise brought into focus. Sometimes, though, one might open the book at random, just to see what the oracle has to say.

Three Natures. Far and away the most common query, "Three Natures" poses one question three times.

1. First to resonate with the world as it seems.
2. Second to resonate with what is intrinsic but not obvious.
3. Third to resonate with possibility.

The Spiral of Nine. An enhanced consultation comes from esoteric tradition, which may arrange this response as a pattern of cards instead of rolling dice. "The Spiral of Nine," actually requires ten casts, the first three of which are substantially the same as "Three Natures."

In sequence, the casts are:

1. A Face
2. The Deeps
3. What Chance
4. A Gate
5. A Choice
6. An Instrument
7. An Ally
8. A Test
9. At Heart
10. An Outlier

Only the questioner can know whether a response bears on the query. Practice is to consider a response in all of its parts, and then go with instinct.

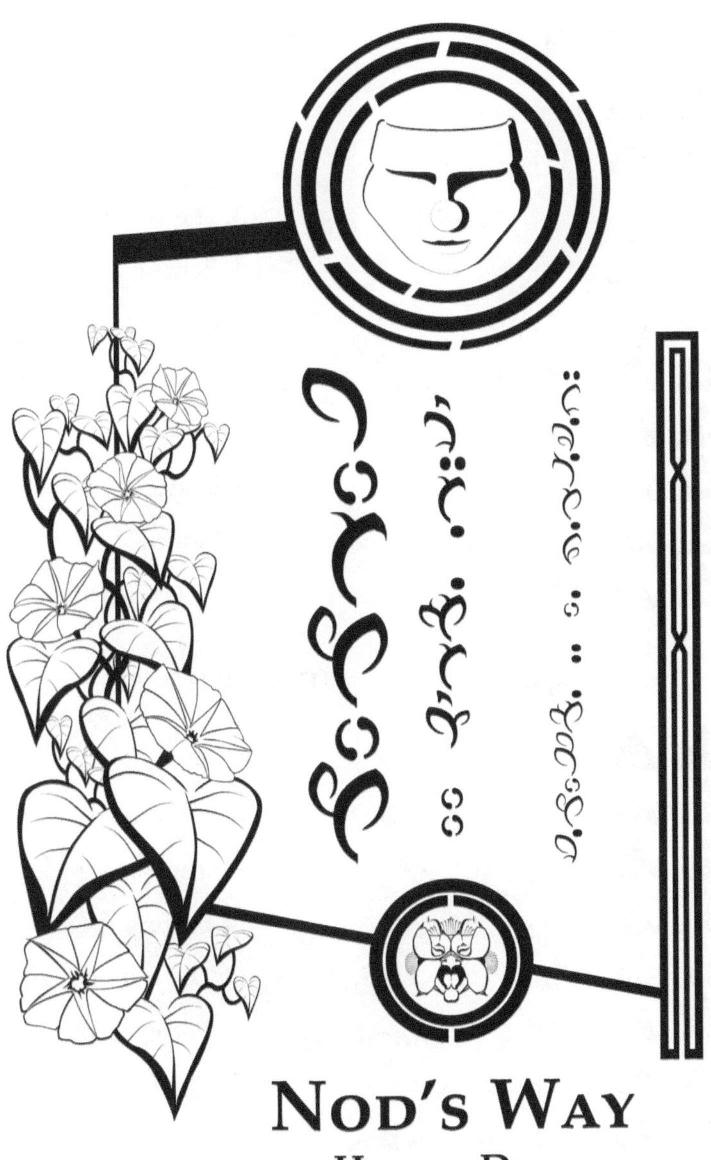

Nod's Way
or Hidden Dragon

an oracle of the everyday

THE MOON HOUSE

THE STAR HOUSE

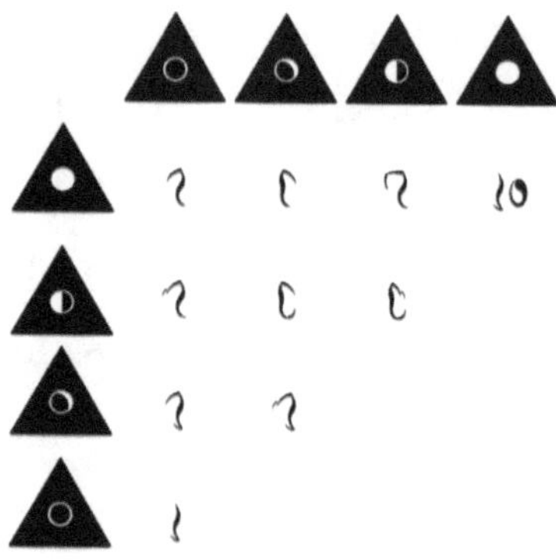

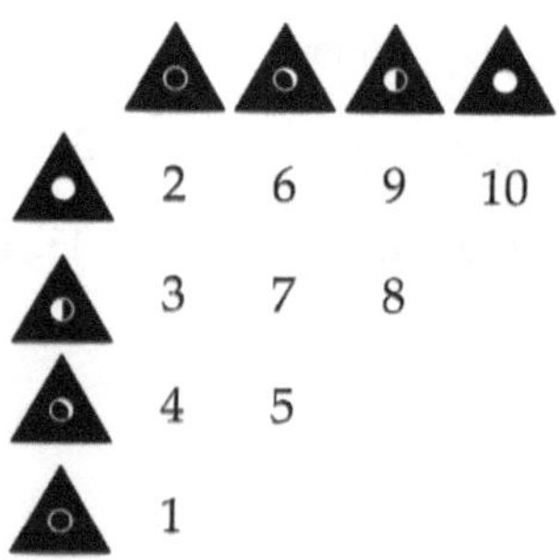

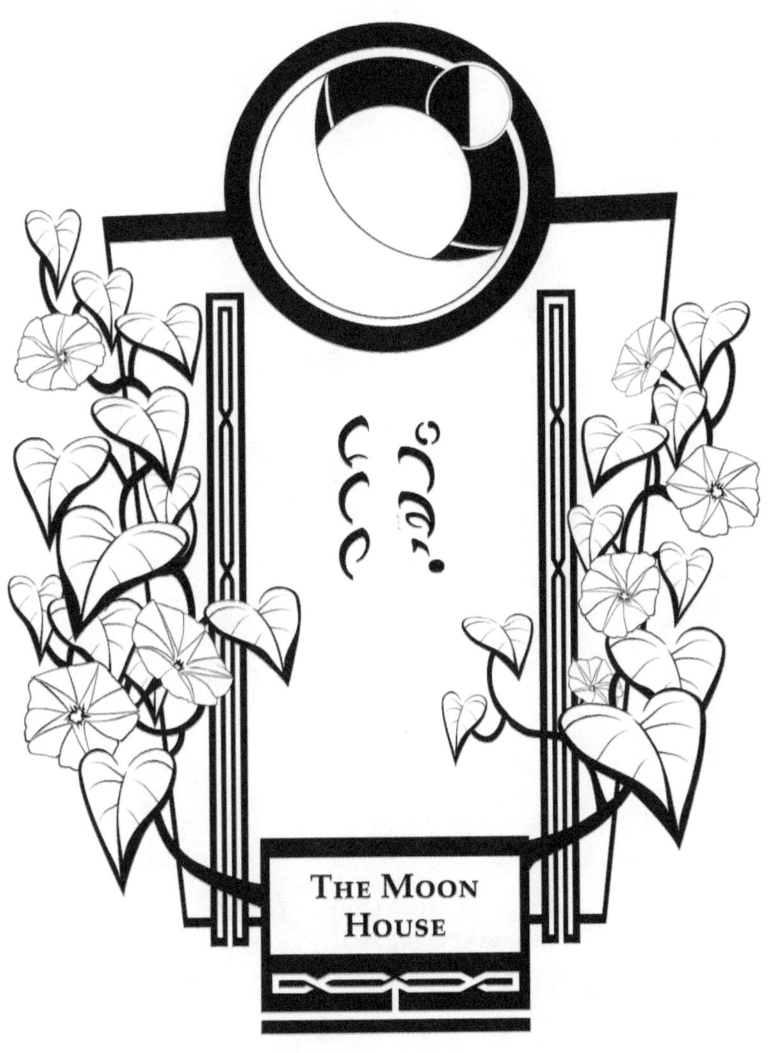

The Moon
House

THE MOON HOUSE

Bright of the Moon
at fullest face,
songbirds wake
surprised and call.

Half Moon lights
an open road,
but skirts the edge
of power's hall.

Crescent skims
the overhead,
able craft
on stellar beams.

Dark of the Moon
sits wise at home,
advances plot or,
dozing, dreams.

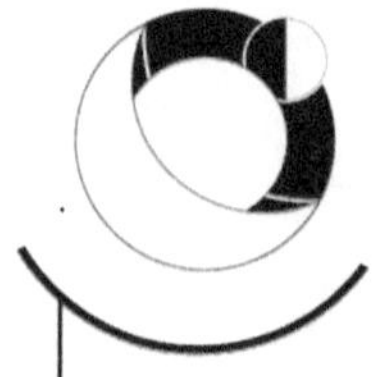

1. WAITING

Dark of the moon to dark of the moon. A cycle of waiting.

Complication—or peril—may color the time, but with patience comes strength to wait. Waiting is not the same as idleness.

Moment by moment, Nod prepares for action.

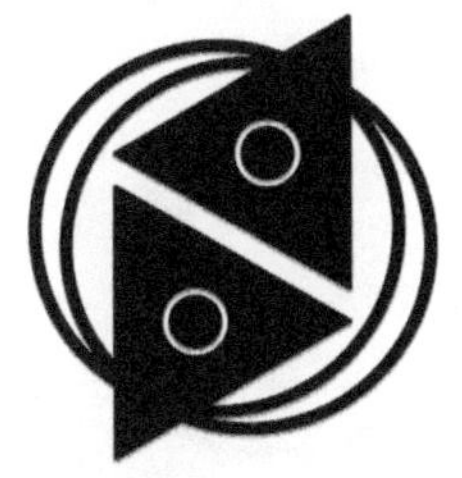

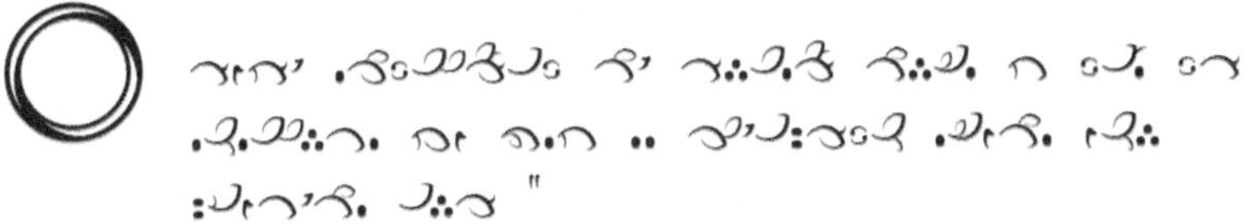

Calendar: 36   (December 12 to December 21)
Resonance: 7
Compass: standing eastsouth

○ If called to release the old and live empty for a time, remain open to the unexpected.

| Do not overreach. Clarity waits within.

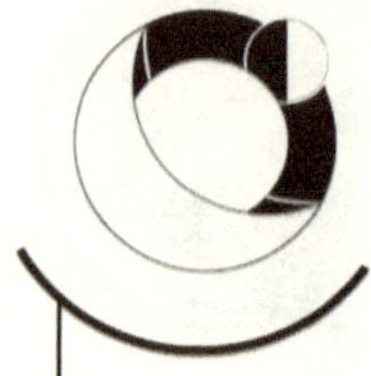

2. TRUST

Dark of the moon and the bright. Trust that what is seen and what is unseen are one.

Honor the seen and the unseen in all things. Do not be surprised by which hand offers in return.

Discarding arrogance, Nod finds balance.

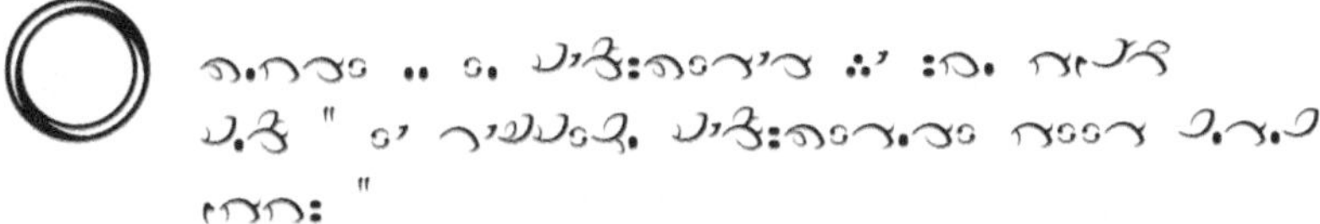

Calendar: 28   (September 23 to October 2)
Resonance: 17
Compass: standing northeast

A time of separations may seem like loss. With trust, separation becomes new freedom.

Give thought to what you trust. If you do not hear and fail to see, opportunity slips away.

3. THE WILD

Half face and dark of the moon. The wild takes new shape wherever it roots. Where unseen, it waits to spring up.

The wild is a flower rising in the path, and the forest in all its diversity. It is the living earth. Watch. Listen.

Nod is wild by example from every side.

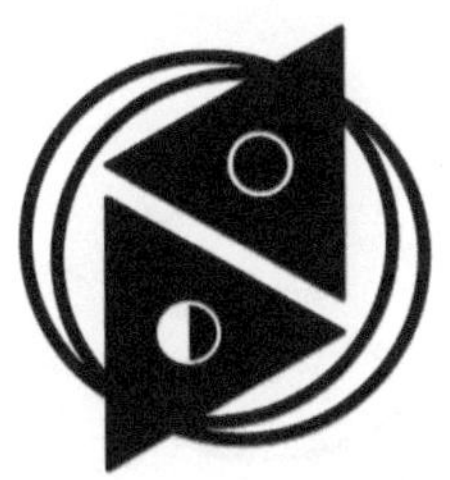

Calendar: 26   (September 2 to September 11)
Resonance: 5
Compass: standing northwest

○ Defend the wild to defend yourself. Times of good fortune, no less than bad, bear watching.

| Amidst total disruption, you must become wild. This is opportunity.

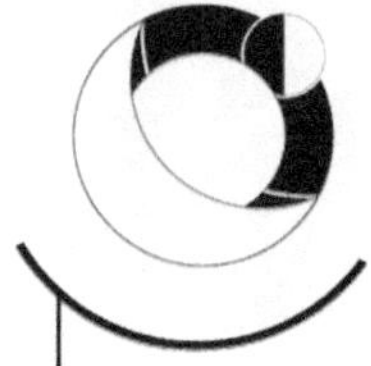

4. RETREAT

Crescent face and dark of the moon. Light enough to retreat, but not enough to stay.

When you cannot hold, do not abandon hope and flee. Prepare for return as you cede the field.

Nod retreats to gather strength.

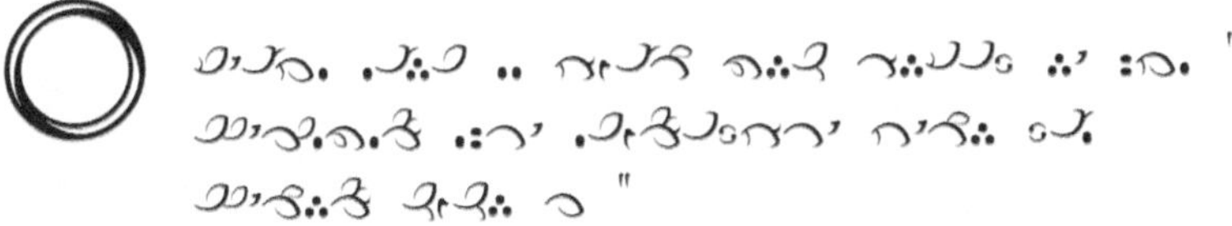

Calendar: 6   (February 11 to February 20)
Resonance: 34
Compass: standing north

○ A great lesson may come disguised as loss. Begin farthest out and work toward home.

❘ Prepare for return by discarding any thing that adds only weight.

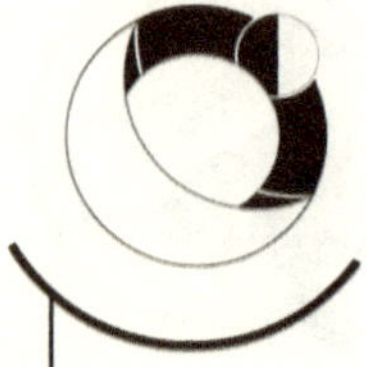

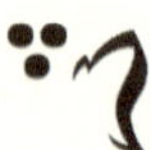

5. JOY

Eyes of delight, like two crescent moons.

A time of joy opens new doors. If these demand rethinking plans, do so with celebration.

Without looking, Nod spies where joy waits.

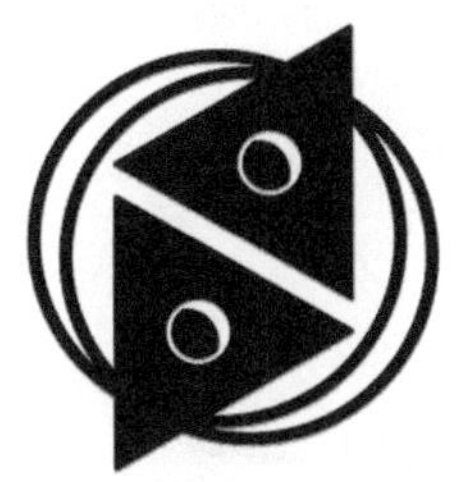

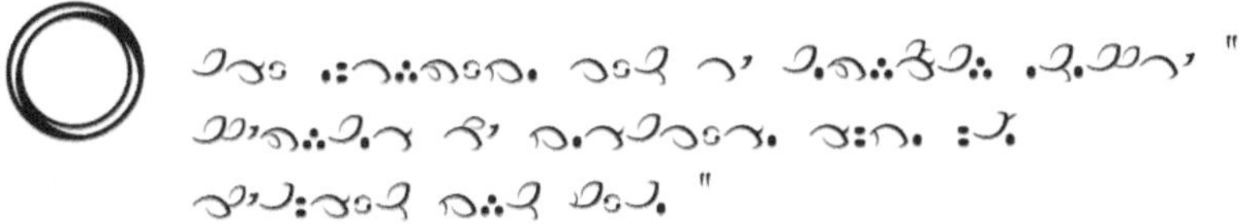

Calendar: 19   (June 24 to July 3)
Resonance: 24
Compass: rising west

Irresponsible joy descends into hollow pleasure. Allow yourself euphoria, but continue to do right.

Release what has been shut away. The veil is a barrier to joy.

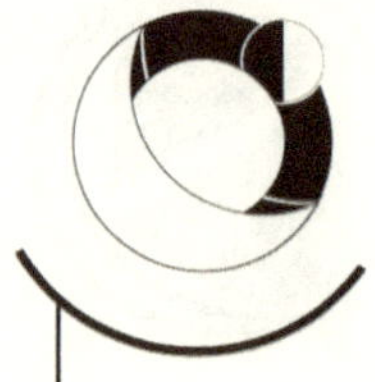

6. DECISIVE ACTION

The full moon is clear mind. The crescent is a blade that slices restraints.

Proceed calmly, without hurry or delay. Ignore desire and shed bias in order to see the road.

Nod moves without hesitation.

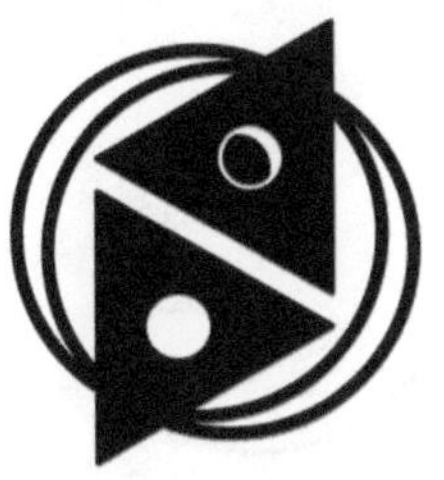

ツ.メ✦.メꝋ ?0

✦ꝋꝋツ.ꝋ:. ?？

ハːツꝋ♪   ゾːメ. ⋅✦ːꝋハːハ.

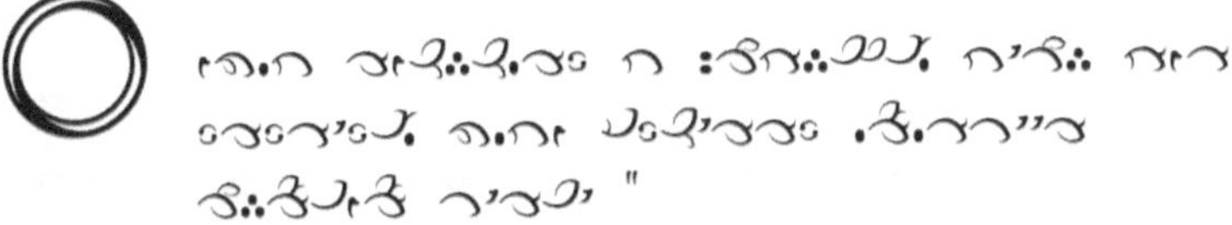

Calendar: 30   (October 13 to October 22)
Resonance: 14
Compass: standing west

◯ When the lightest touch changes everything, sharp eyes
   serve well.

❘ Capable action spies obstacles and moves through them
   like wind.

19

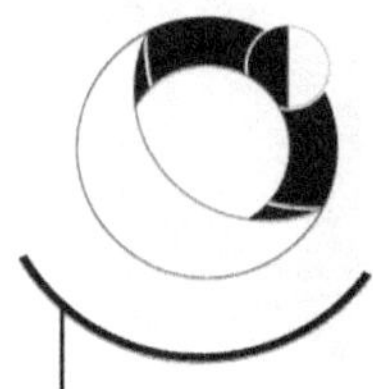

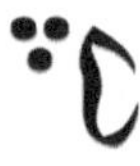

7. SEEKING

Half moon and crescent. Meshing pieces suggest the whole.

Parts assemble, some from within, some from without. What is missing in one may nest in others. Answers may wait at home.

Nod finds no benefit chasing around.

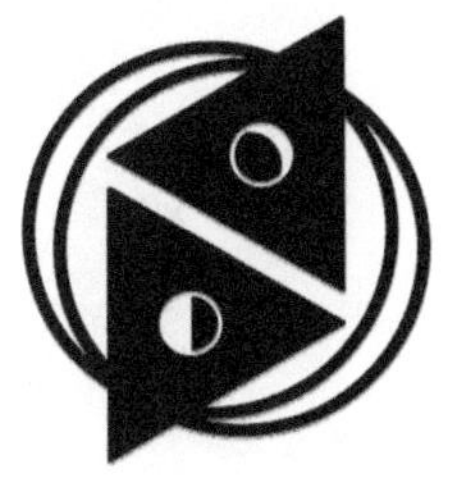

ᘓ.ᐟ.ᔭ.ᐟ.ᕲᕲ ??

ᔭₒᕲᕲᐝ.ᔭᕲ∵ I?

ᐠ∶ᔭₒᐝᐝ   ᕲ∶ᐟ. ᐧᐠᘁᐝᐧ.

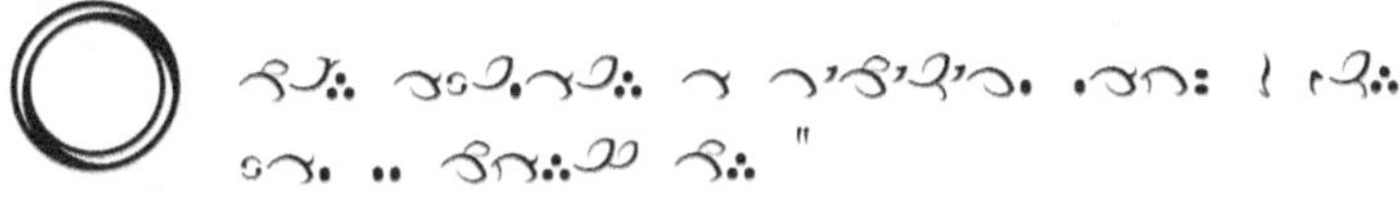

○ ᔭᐟ∴ ᔭₒᕲᐧᐠᕲ∴ ᐧ ᐧᐧᔭᐧᔭᐧᕲ. ᐧᔭᐠ∶ � ⎮ ᘁᕲ∴
   ᕲᐧ. .. ᔭᐠ∴ᕲ ᔭ∴ "

⎮ ᕲᐧᔭ∶ᐟᕲ ᐠᕲᐠᕲᕲᐝᐝᐧ ᐧᐧ ᕲ.ᕲᔭ∶ᐠᕲ "
   ᔭᕲᕲᕲ∶ᕲ.ᕲᕲ∴.ᕲᕲ ᐧ ᐝ∶ᔭᐧᕲ.ᐝᔭ. ∶ᔭᐝ "

Calendar: 32   (November 2 to November 11)
Resonance: 19
Compass: falling west

○ Seeking partnership is but one gate to a larger life.

⎮ Resist collapse into emotion. Thoughtlessness is not
   immersion.

8. UNITY

Two half moons. Together they shine fully.

Unity neither flatters nor oppresses. Learn from error and forgive misstep. Companions rise with purpose.

Nod and Nods: harmony in one voice.

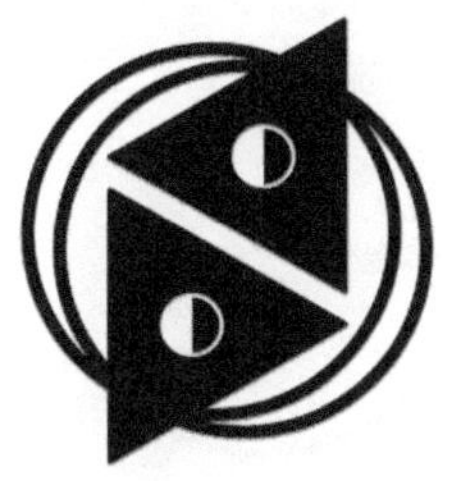

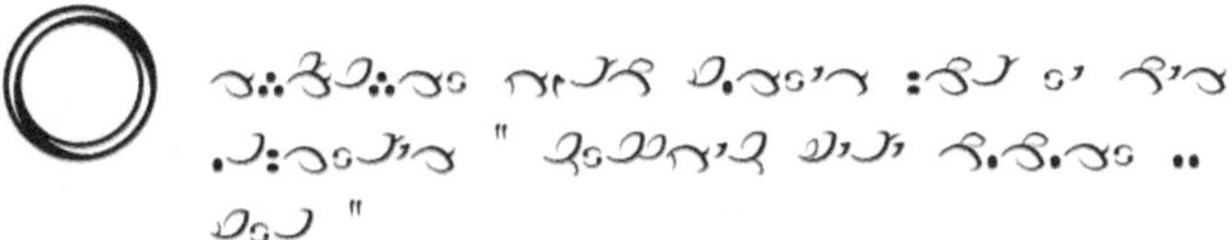

Calendar: 15   (May 13 to May 22)
Resonance: 15
Compass: rising southwest

Unity may not accord with private aims. Even a just cause negotiates.

Act not only as an individual, but as hands and eyes of a larger life.

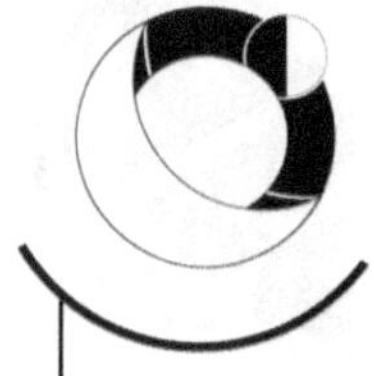

9. RETURN

Return. Brighter than before by half.

Darkness recedes in the hour of transformation. Release the stale and return anew. Possibility hides in familiar shadows.

Nod watches habit in the act to find the Dragon.

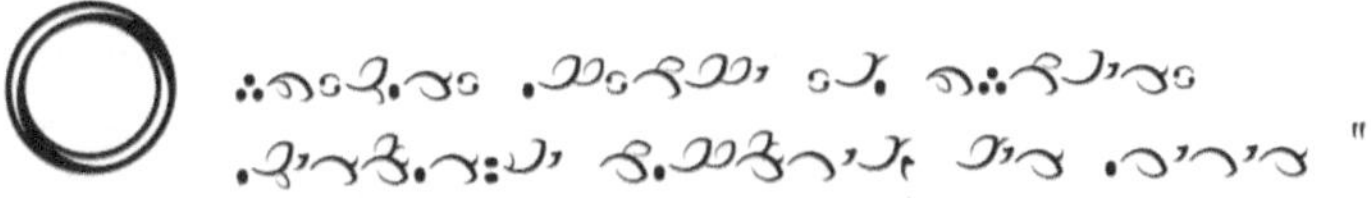

Calendar: 21   (July 14 to July 23)
Resonance: 31
Compass: standing east

○ Quiet Return and a modest profile bridge rough waters.

| Returning again and again. Too often drains the well.

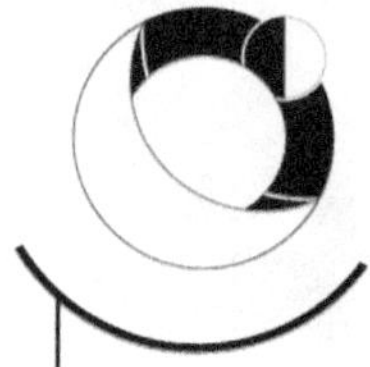

10. THE GUARDIAN

Bright of the moon to bright of the moon. A guardian is called to stand ready.

A guardian cares for garden, acknowledges custom, and protects the wild. This is ground for relationship.

Nod tends where needed.

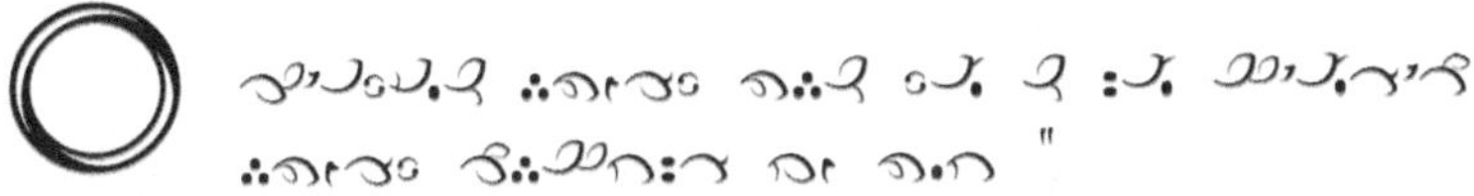

Calendar: 13   (April 23 to May 2)
Resonance: 8
Compass: standing southwest

○ Observe what comes and goes, but insist on what abides.

| Steady. Do not be sucked under by rushes of old while preparing for new.

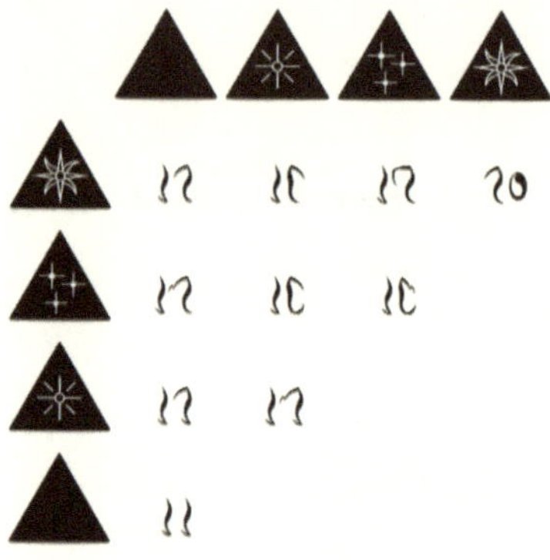

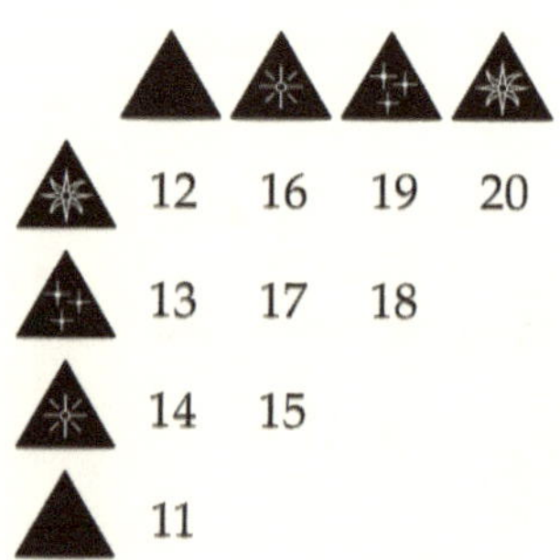

12 16 19 20
13 17 18
14 15
11

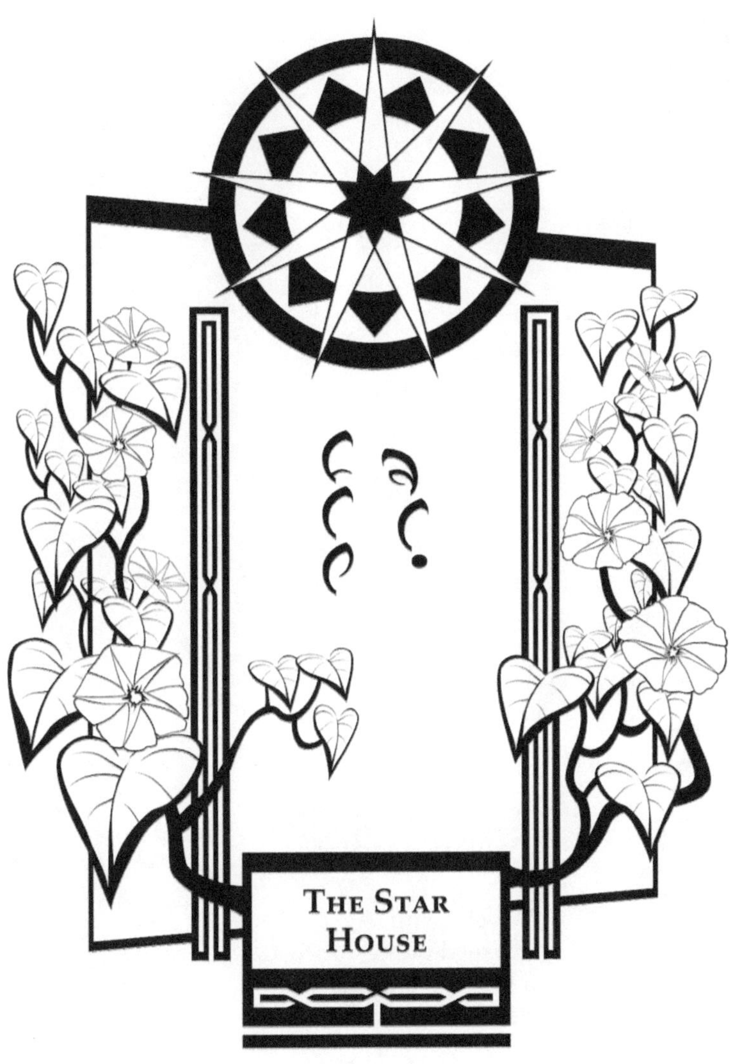

THE STAR
HOUSE

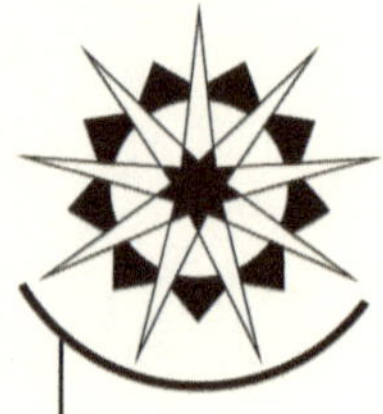

THE STAR HOUSE

Daystar, sun,
the seed of life,
a grain in endless
fields of dark.

The Myriads,
across the black like dust,
each fiery speck
an engine sparks.

Starburst, brilliant,
storms and fades,
what flames so hot
does not endure.

The Void holds all,
itself a maze,
enfolding, folded,
vastness pure.

11. BUILDING

Void on all sides. There are no limits by which to measure.

When light cannot shine, lay foundations where you stand. Building shelters new life as it hatches. Still, building cannot be continuous or unrestrained.

The Dragon breathes by push and pull.

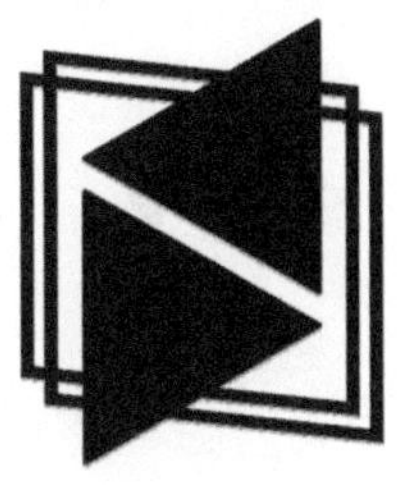

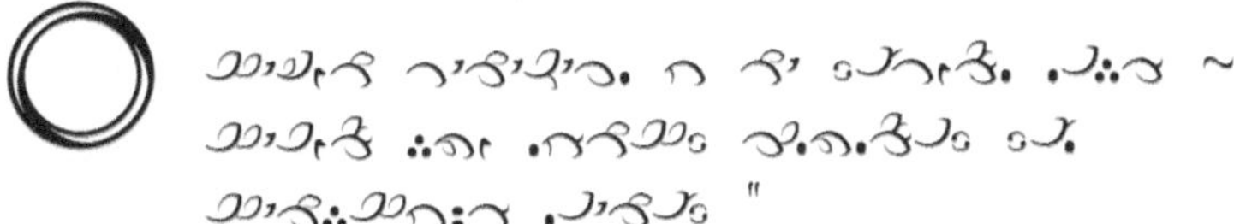

Calendar: 25   (August 23 to September 1)
Resonance: 22
Compass: rising eastsouth

○ Open the gate for increase. Complete what you have begun and stand ready.

| Go deeply into things with diligence. Do not resist a task at hand.

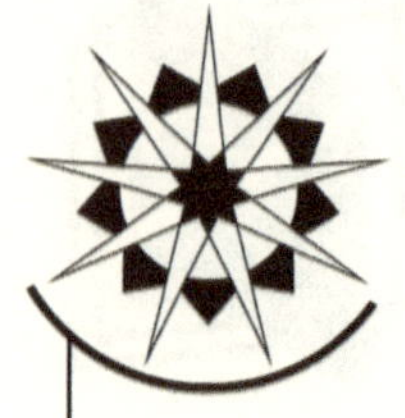

12. GENEROSITY

**Daystar and void. The sun blazing in the vessel of space.
Generous when it acts, it is tolerant when it stays its hand.**

Generosity creates conditions that feed others, and welcomes able
counsel.

Generous Nod discovers abundance.

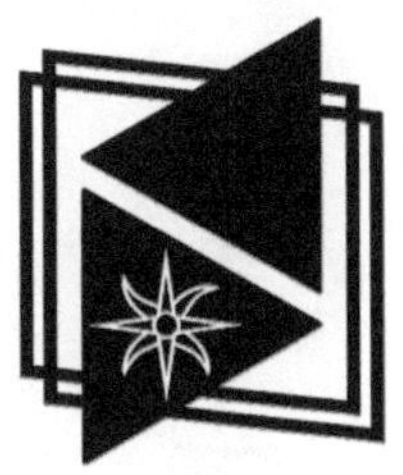

Calendar: 33   (November 12 to November 21)
Resonance: 6
Compass: rising northeast

If you are blocked, know it may be your own missed step.
Be generous. Each moment begins anew.

Feed others to feed yourself.

35

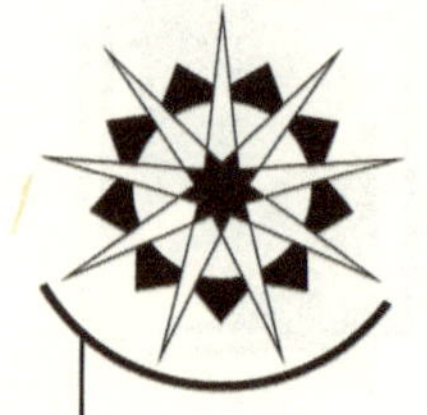

13. THE SIMPLE

The myriad stars, the vastness of space. Beside these what boast?

Progress often moves by means and through ways of simplicity. If thought is pushed too far, the chance to act is lost.

Nod completes what must be done with simple ornament.

Calendar: 24   (August 13 to August 22)
Resonance: 30
Compass: rising southeast

Quiet change goes unremarked.

Major change strips away the purely decorative. Retain
what feeds the spirit.

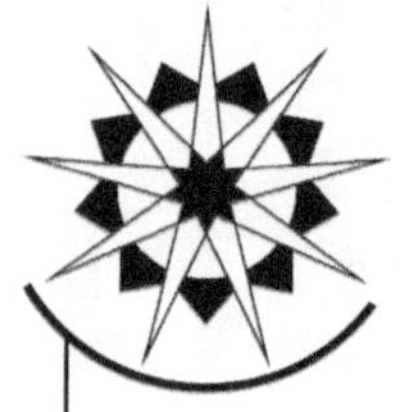

14. SORROW

Starburst and void. A flash in the dark, then absence that lingers.

Weep until the stream runs dry. In sorrow, feelings are more necessary than expectations. Focus on what is nearest and attend to what requires it.

When tears have finished, they stop.

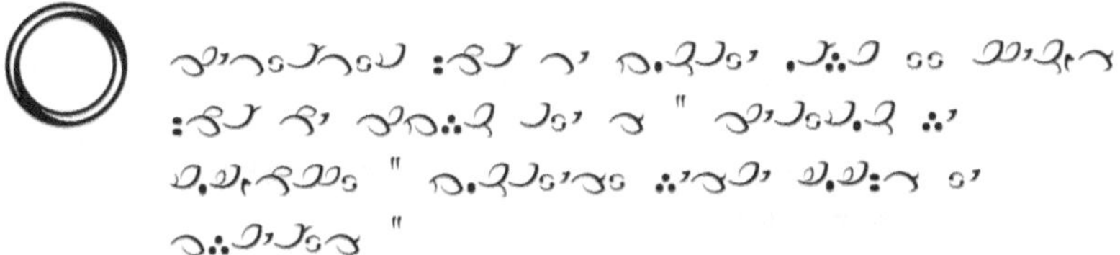

Calendar: 20   (July 4 to July 13)
Resonance: 32
Compass: rising south

○ Do not give over to great sorrow or try to avoid it. Watch as you feel. Sorrow, too, fades with distance.

❘ Put your house in order or court sorrow. Look within even as you look out.

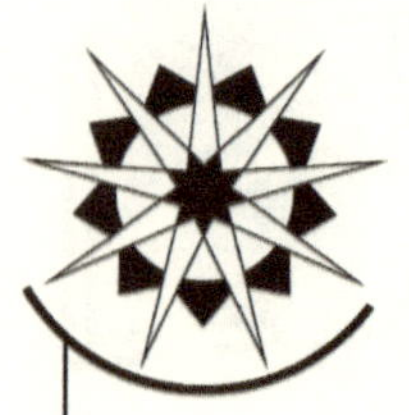

15. DISRUPTION

Two bursting stars. Look out! Upheaval arrives.

Disruption frightens, but this is not bad. After facing terrors within, those without lose power. Do not fight obstructions blindly. Consider how to shape them.

Nod deflects the burst, then lends a hand.

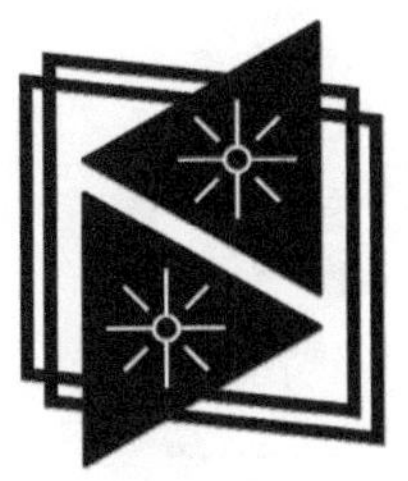

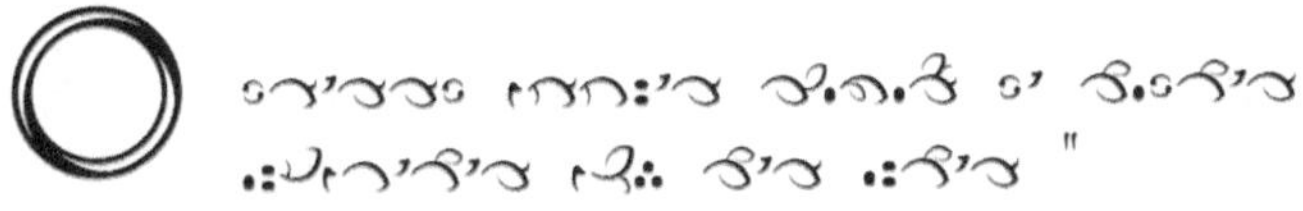

Calendar: 11   (April 3 to April 12)
Resonance: 1
Compass: standing south

New lives begin with unexpected turns onto unsought paths.

You yourself influence what is happening. Adapt.

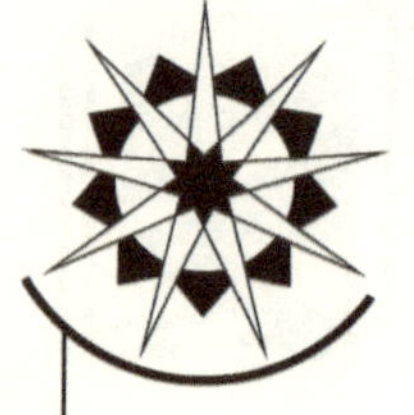

16. PERSEVERANCE

Daystar and starburst. Abiding sun grows life in season; a flash in the void makes future promise.

Persevere in your chosen part, undistracted by chatter of fashion. When thrill is spent, perseverance continues.

Sour or sweet, Nod perseveres.

Calendar: 8   (March 3 to March 12)
Resonance: 10
Compass: falling southeast

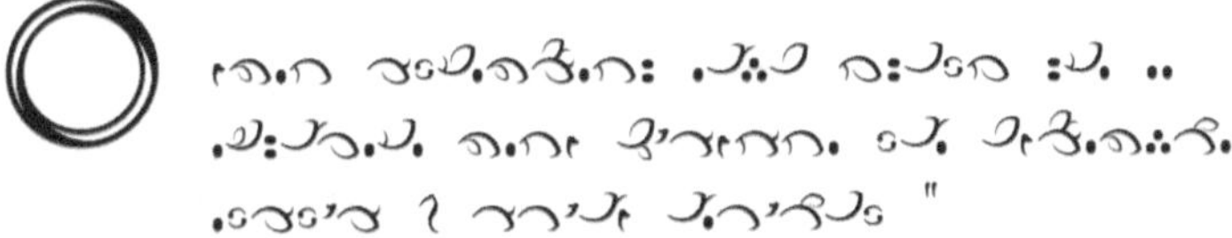

When the Great Teacher dons adversity's mask, creativity and perseverance both are needed.

Do not abandon perseverance if you lapse. Name the cause, learn the lesson, and begin again.

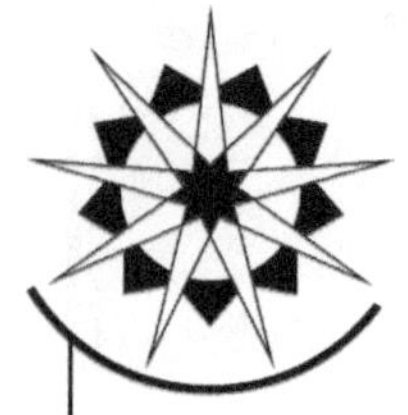

17. THE EARTH

Starburst among myriads. A flash in the scape, a flicker in the arms of night, nameless, this earth.

The real mystery is not hidden, but dances on every side. Leading the earth trips into peril. Following brings bountiful reward.

Nod follows, taking nothing by force.

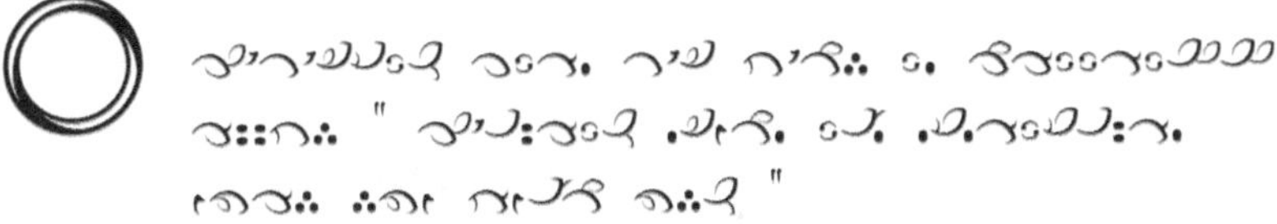

Calendar: 3   (January 12 to January 21)
Resonance: 25
Compass: standing southeast

○ Trust your own best nature. Remain open and sincere, come what may.

❘ Do not seek the moment, but take one when it presents itself. Trust; do not anticipate.

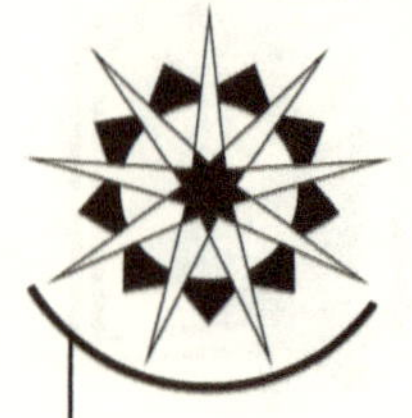

18. THE COLLECTIVE

A myriad myriads together in time. Gifts emerge in numbers.

By adding the collective multiplies. Stand firm for what nourishes the larger life—in friendship, not by force.

Nod with Nods decides.

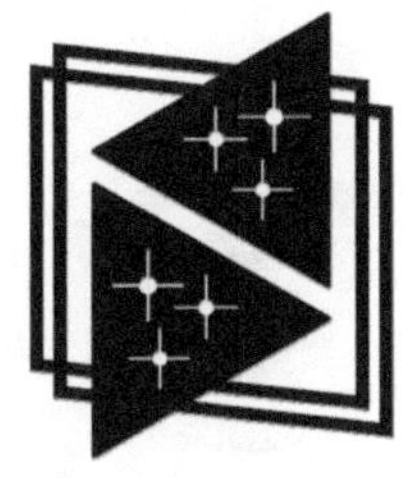

Calendar: 5   (February 1 to February 10)
Resonance: 4
Compass: falling eastsouth

The collective calls forth patience, perseverance,
cooperation, courage and plans for whatever follows.

When at last you understand what you know, the bounty
already yours will shine.

47

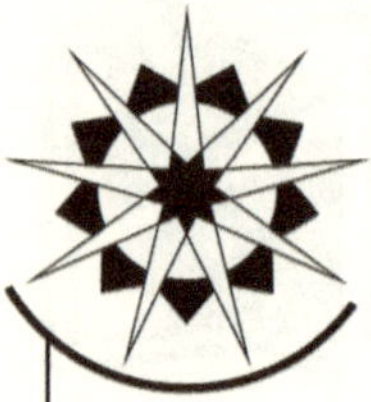

19. THE SKY

Daystar and its cousins of the starry night. The province of sky.

The sky is a realm of unrestricted movement, with access through every dimension. Undertakings pursued to the end bring great benefit.

Nod shines with imagination.

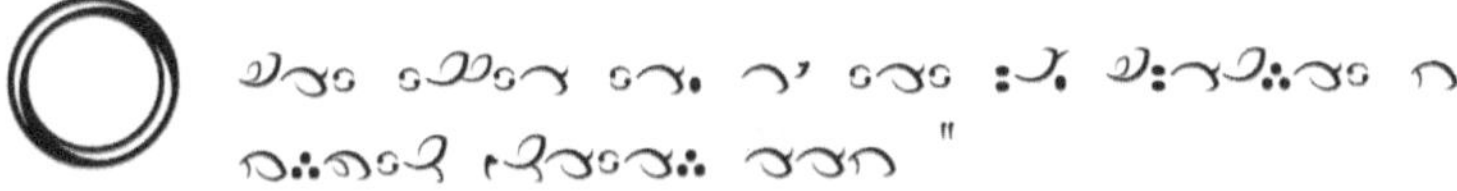

Calendar: 2   (January 2 to January 11)
Resonance: 28
Compass: rising eastnorth

Light breathes life into all, but the dark holds us together.

Examine motives with light on every side, and adjust your attitude.

49

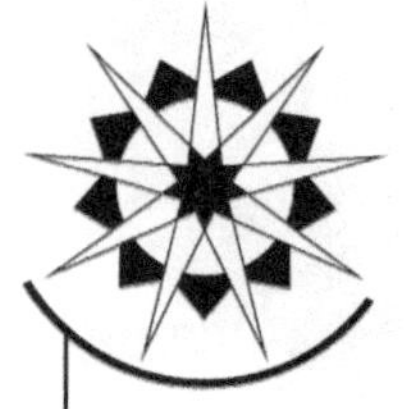

20. GENTLENESS

Daystar to daystar. In the cycle of days, gentleness abides in great power.

The effect of gentleness is gradual. Moment by moment one sees no fruit. A quiet voice overtakes commanding acts.

Nod meshes gently and finds an ear.

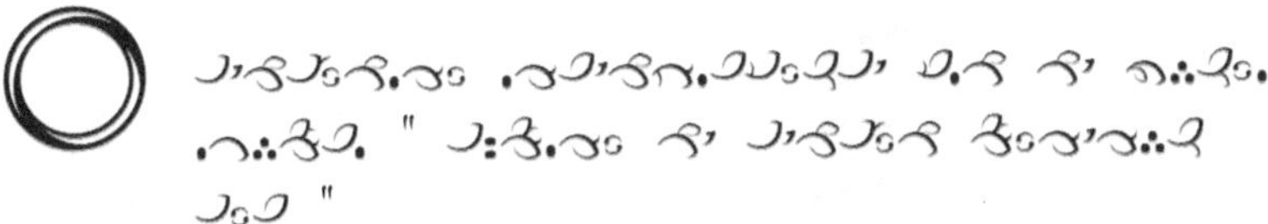

Calendar: 17   (June 3 to June 12)
Resonance: 9
Compass: falling south

○ Careful preparation invites gentle effect. Failure to prepare
courts trouble.

❘ Be at ease, undistracted by absent voices. Gently follow
your chosen track.

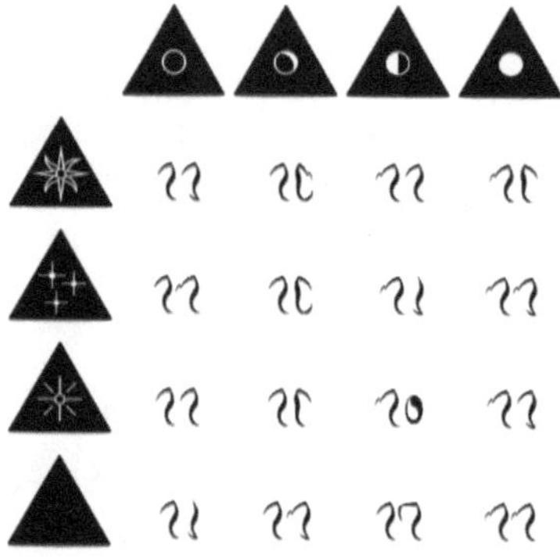

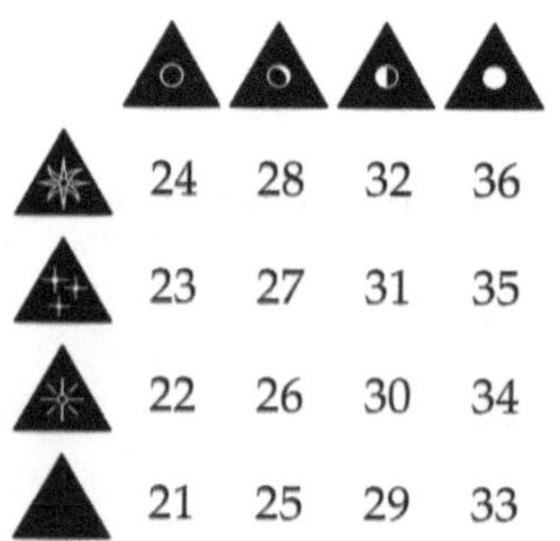

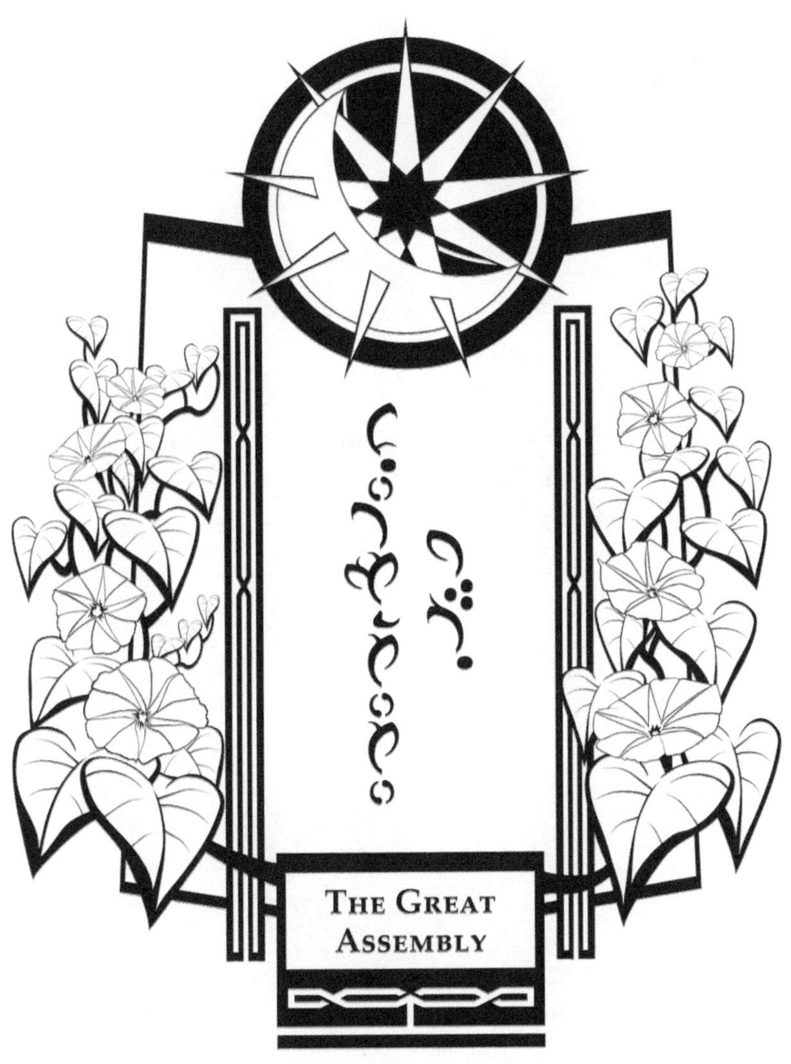

THE GREAT
ASSEMBLY

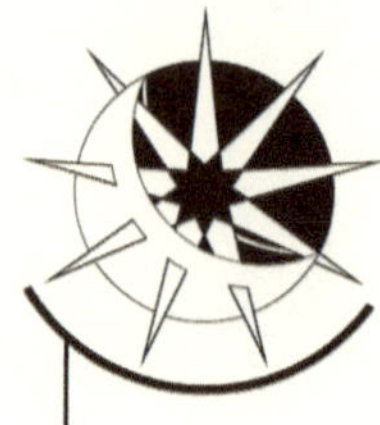

THE GREAT ASSEMBLY

Star with moon
some portents link,
To swear by moon
and wish on star.

The steadfast pearl
a metric makes;
suns flame or fade,
grow cold or char.

In dreams of life,
the stars abide;
seed the void,
soon sprouts a throng.

Mute companion
times the tides;
moon sets the beat,
stars sing the song.

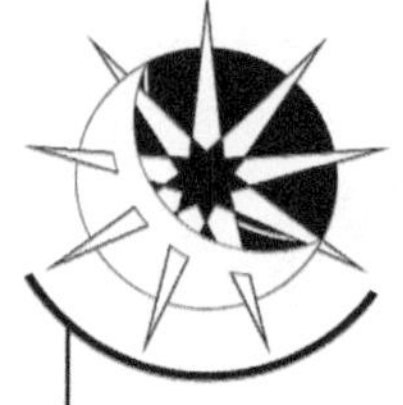

21. STAND STILL

Dark of the moon and the void of night. The road degenerates; opportunity declines.

Collapse negates any action. When darkness covers all, rest and observe the cycle. Standing still is the face of future movement.

Nod's wait is matter of fact.

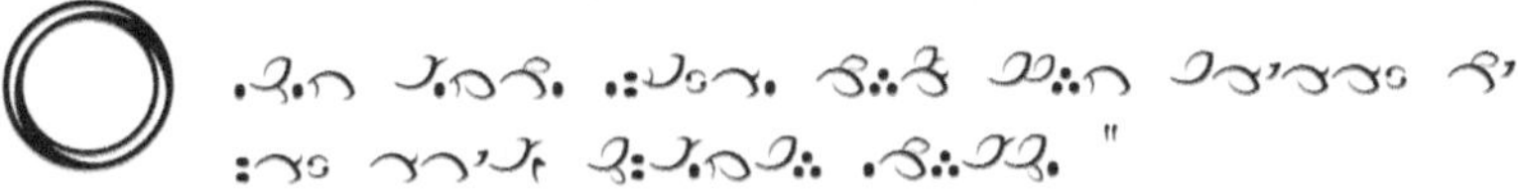

Calendar: 12   (April 13 to April 22)
Resonance: 33
Compass: falling northwest

○ Where invisible influence works, sacrifice is powerful
   resistence.

| Before attempting to exceed your reach, draw breath and
   measure first.

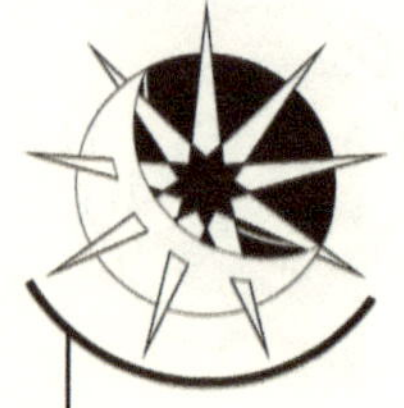

22. SELF RELIANCE

Dark of the moon, a flash in the sky. Conditions are governed not from within but from without.

When barriers rise, surprises will happen. Assistance is not certain. Should opportunity arise, do not become drunk with increase.

Nod's fortune wilts without diligence.

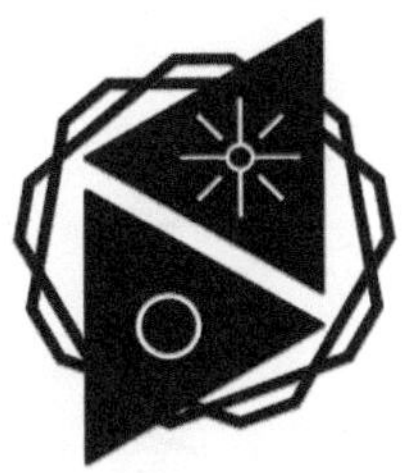

Calendar: 35   (December 2 to December 11)
Resonance: 16
Compass: rising westnorth

Pause to reflect on where you stand with yourself, but seize opportunity when it is at hand.

Look sharp! Stepping with empty hands toward accomplishment, do not grow careless.

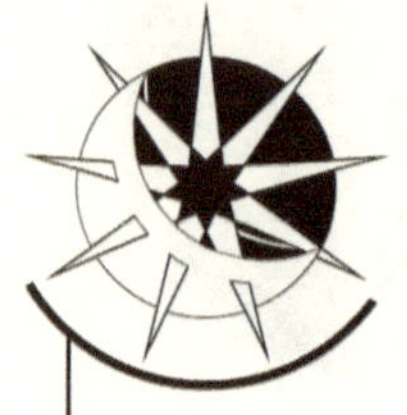

23. FOLLY

Dark of the moon and starry night. By the small lights of one mind.

Step into the world with eyes shut and meet the Great Teacher.
A confident fool fails promise. A careless fool is blind to chance.
A fool by design may prevail.

Ignoring the lure, Nod avoids the tangle.

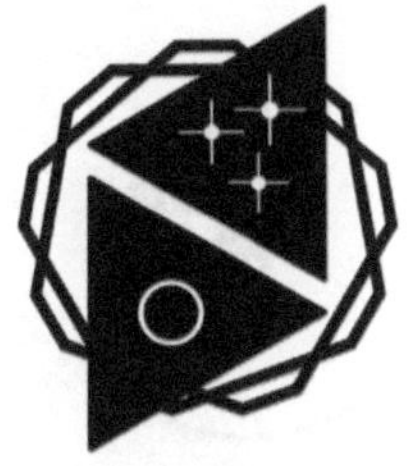

Calendar: 23   (August 3 to August 12)
Resonance: 36
Compass: falling north

○ Hatching folly calls for patience. A light touch sways what has not taken shape.

| Departing from the old demands honesty, though you appear a fool.

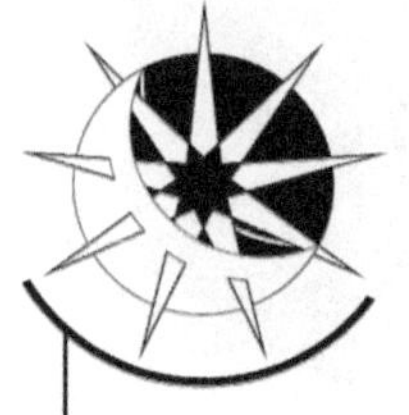

24. REPAIR

Daystar after dark of the moon. There is light to repair what has been spoiled.

What has been spoiled through act or neglect can be repaired. Outcome depends on care and preparation.

Nod measures twice and works until finished.

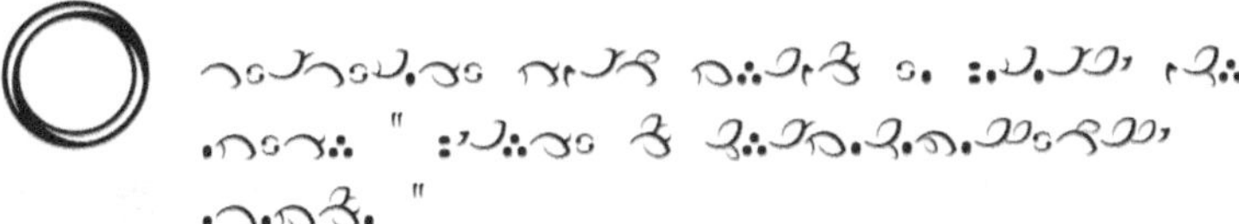

Calendar: 14   (May 3 to May 12)
Resonance: 21
Compass: falling northeast

○ Breakdown may range from unimportant to serious. None of it makes frustration productive.

| Tackle the biggest challenge first: admit what you would rather not admit. Everything afterward will be easier.

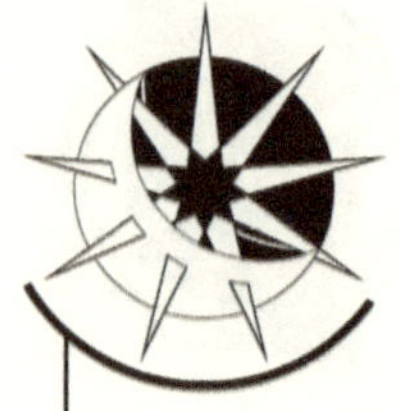

25. MODESTY

Crescent transits The Void. Modesty. Enough without more.

Modesty is Hidden Dragon. In fortune, modesty adorns the wise.
Loose in the world, it draws regard.

Without boasting or seeking praise, Nod continues.

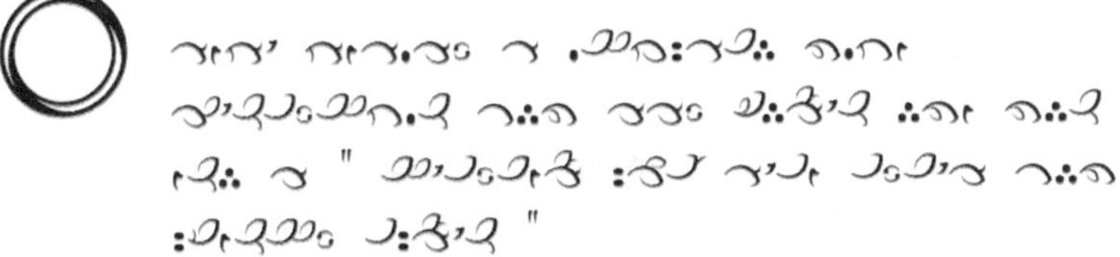

Calendar: 31   (October 23 to November 1)
Resonance: 13
Compass: falling westsouth

If change is painful, recall that it reflects what comes to it. Do not fret over unavoidable trials.

Even with outcome assured, the cycle must complete. Be firm but patient with process. Be modest in the world.

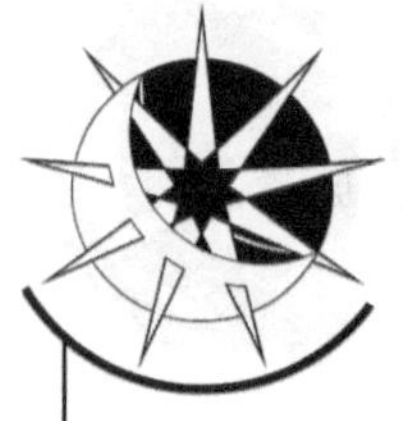

26. COURAGE

Crescent and bursting star. Quiet courage across cycles of days; bright courage in dire moments.

No matter how challenge begins, courage helps secure the end. Purpose and spirit drive timely action. Temperance and courtesy perfect it.

Nod rises when called.

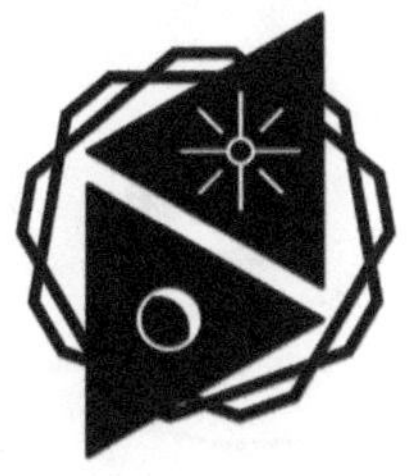

Calendar: 18   (June 13 to June 22)
Resonance: 12
Compass: falling eastnorth

Read the face of the Great Teacher in events, and defeat is never complete.

The task for its own sake! Lust after outcomes and courage may fail.

27. INNOCENCE

Crescent moon and starry night. Clear mind, without base motives.

Become innocent. Act not for gain but to sustain the world.

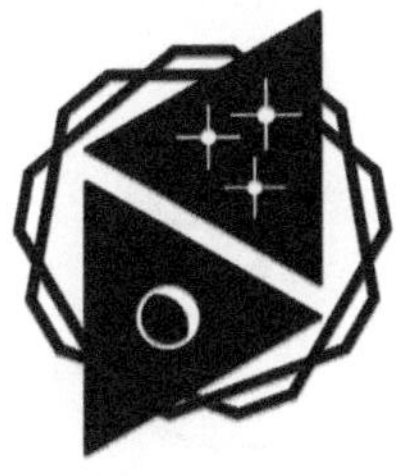

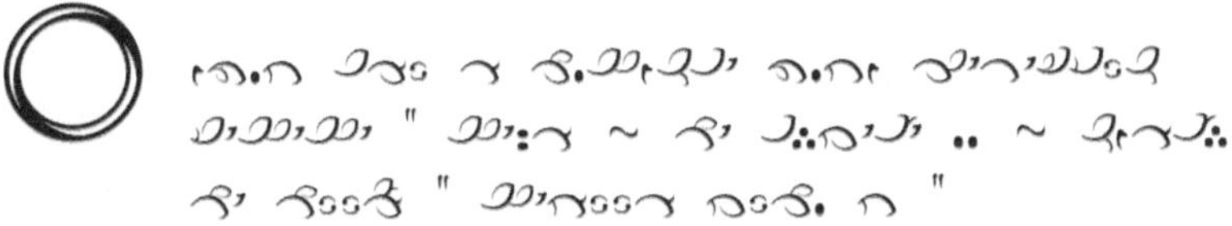

Calendar: 9   (March 13 to March 22)
Resonance: 18
Compass: rising north

When joy is afoot, trust intuition. Cease, for a moment, trying to understand. Become the dance.

Clear thoughts of conflict. Observe the day. Proceed without haste.

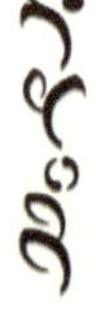

28. REST

The crescent moon pales in the glare of day. Conditions block the path forward.

Looking outside for center, a searcher wanders between joy and sorrow. Instead, get quiet and rest. Rest is rarely mere idleness.

Nod gathers strength and clear mind.

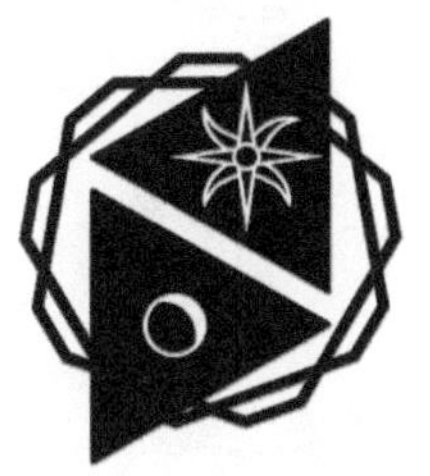

Calendar: 4   (January 22 to January 31)
Resonance: 2
Compass: standing eastnorth

○ When the Great Teacher bides, stand apart and wait.
Prepare the ground on which you stand.

| Storm! Unresolved past will seize control. Be still to find
the blockage. Listen.

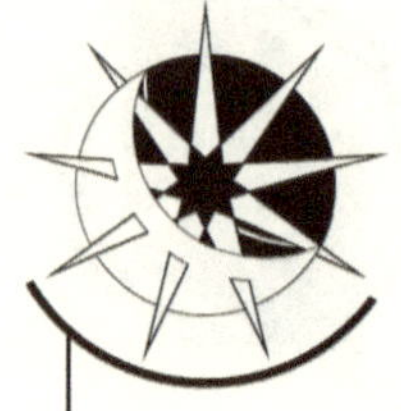

29. THE PARTNER

Half moon brilliant against The Void. As much seen as unseen.

With a partner, light hides as much as it reveals. This is a condition of fact, not choice.

Nod meets halfway in great questions and negotiates small things honestly.

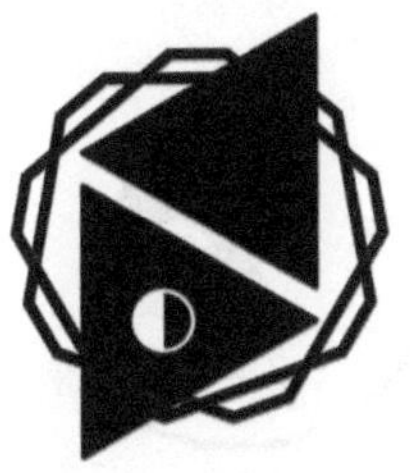

Calendar: 29   (October 3 to October 12)
Resonance: 29
Compass: rising northwest

○ When union is proposed, think hard about whether it can nourish you. Act without haste.

❘ Do not cede everything to union. Partnership must not erase other connections.

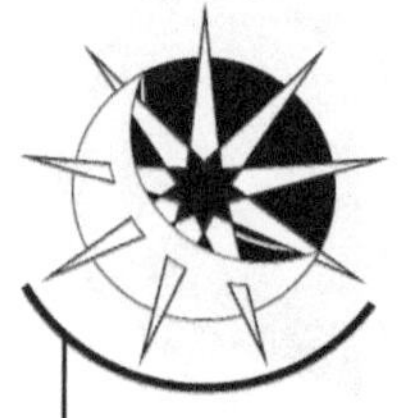

30. RELATIONS

Half moon and starburst. Glimpsed in the normal course; remembered whole in flashes.

Relations within family reflect relations in society. Both are nourished by connection made or born.

Kin ground the Dragon in community and the world.

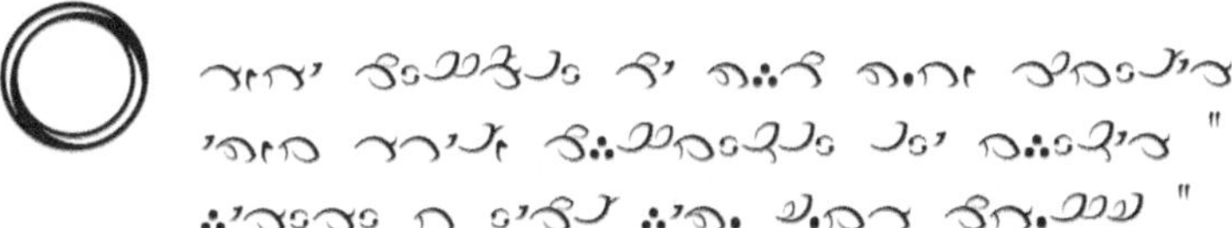

Calendar: 27   (September 12 to September 21)
Resonance: 35
Compass: standing westnorth

If called upon, words must be backed by deeds. The first without the second says little.

Share in the nourishment you give away. Be alert. Anything can happen.

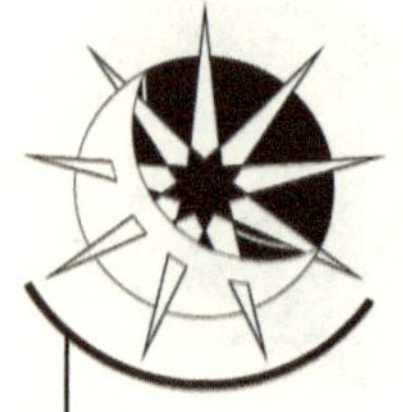

31. MERCY

Half moon and starry night. Merciful illumination.

Mercies received are not always tender. Succor those in need. The reward of mercy is a full heart.

Nod does not begrudge forgiveness.

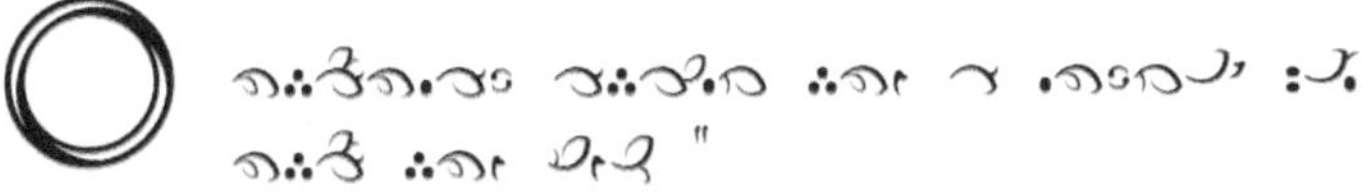

Calendar: 34   (November 22 to December 1)
Resonance: 11
Compass: falling westnorth

Mercy pays what it owes but forgives what it can.

Embrace those who come forward. Let those who do not go in peace.

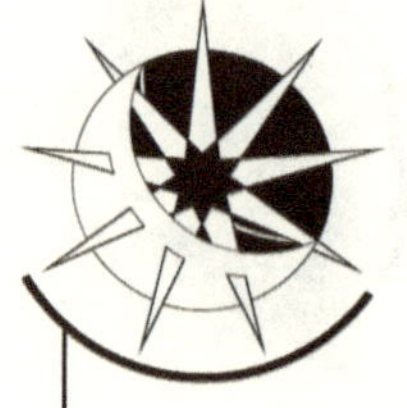

32. THE GARDEN

Half moon shares the day to look upon the garden.

Any place where life abides, a garden of some kind will thrive.
Discover the garden trying to come into being.

A Dragon's garden feeds eyes and spirit.

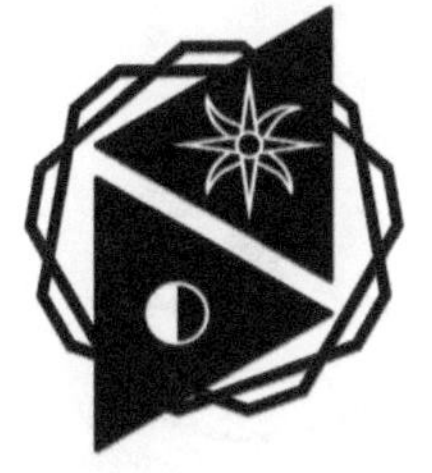

Calendar: 7   (February 21 to March 2)
Resonance: 27
Compass: rising east

Make adversity the silk purse of invention. Every garden needs its wild.

To complete good fortune, share it.

79

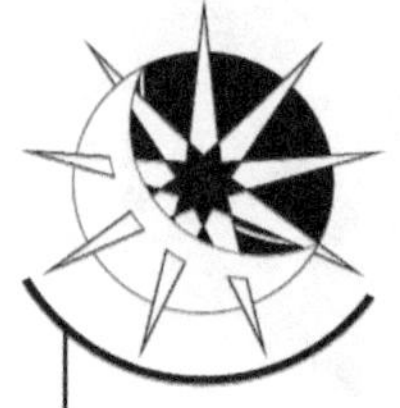

33. THE STEWPOT

Bright of the moon, full in the night.

Values of flesh must defer to spirit, but spirit is formless without flesh. When nourishing spirit, remember flesh. When nourishing self, remember others.

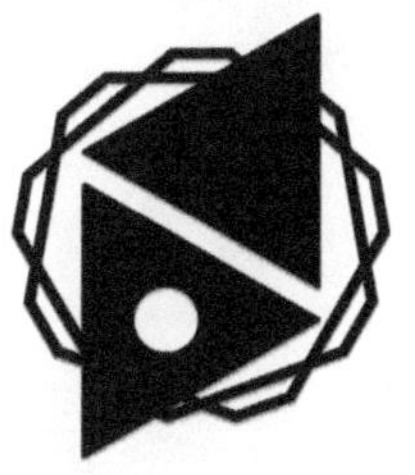

Calendar: 10   (March 24 to April 2)
Resonance: 3
Compass: standing westsouth

Mixing, moving, making connections, transformation simmers.

Don't tread on your own toes and spill the pot.

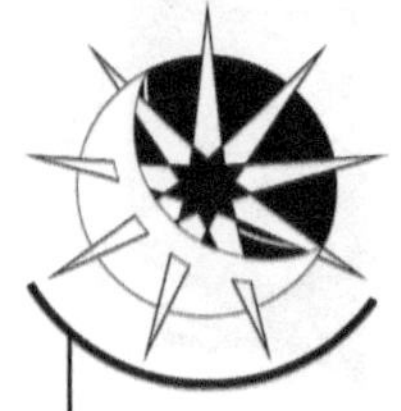

34. STRENGTH

Bright of the moon and bursting star. Explosive strength and strength that endures.

Exceptional conditions call for exceptional response. Bursting strength conquers for a moment, and fades. Enduring strength advances by gentle perseverance.

Nod waits to spy the Dragon and then does not hesitate.

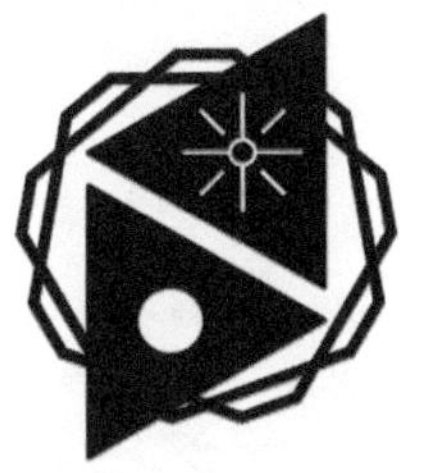

Calendar: 22   (July 24 to August 2)
Resonance: 26
Compass: falling southwest

When all you assume is questioned, enduring strength will sustain.

Life outgrowing old shapes can seem like loss. With new skin comes new strength.

35. COMPLETION

Bright of the moon in the starry night. The old now leads into shadows.

On a broken road, eyes will adjust to see a way forward, but clocks are ticking. Closing one cycle and opening another demands sharp attention.

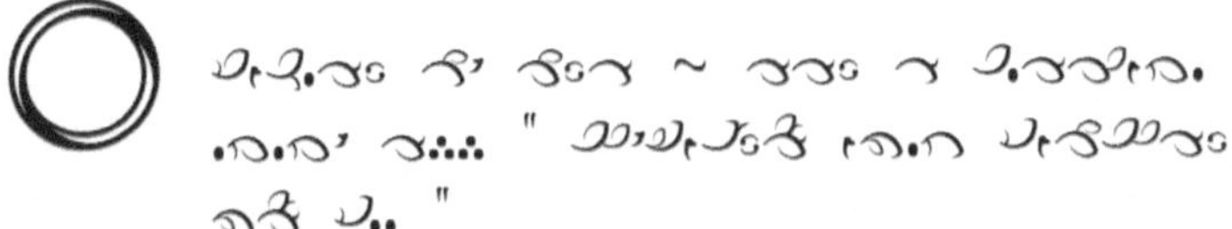

Calendar: 1   (December 23 to January 1)
Resonance: 23
Compass: rising westsouth

Adaptability is its own reward. Respond when chance signals.

If the spring is blocked, you must clean it. If the drain clogs, what is outdated collects around your feet.

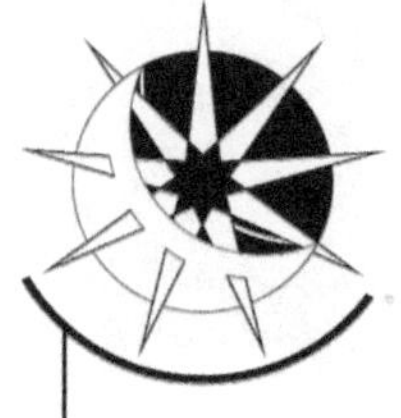

36. THE MYSTERY

Full moon at noon. What we cannot know is always before us.

Pregnant with influence and quick with life, what cannot be known holds boundless potential. This is the secret that explodes all certainty.

Nod finds a key in doubt.

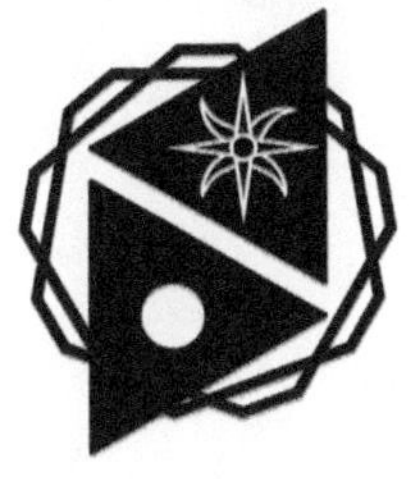

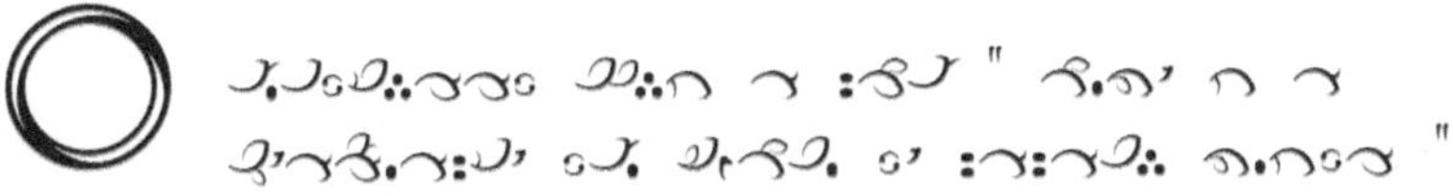

Calendar: 16   (May 24 to June 2)
Resonance: 20
Compass: falling east

○ There is no mystery. The rule is modesty and courage, with diligence, always.

| To enter mystery, give up control. Deep fears fade when exposed to light.

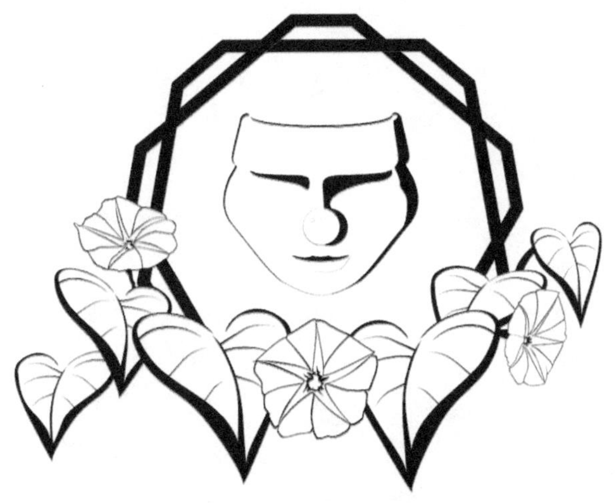

Lenses

ౘౙౚౝౘౙౝౚ   **Numeric Values**

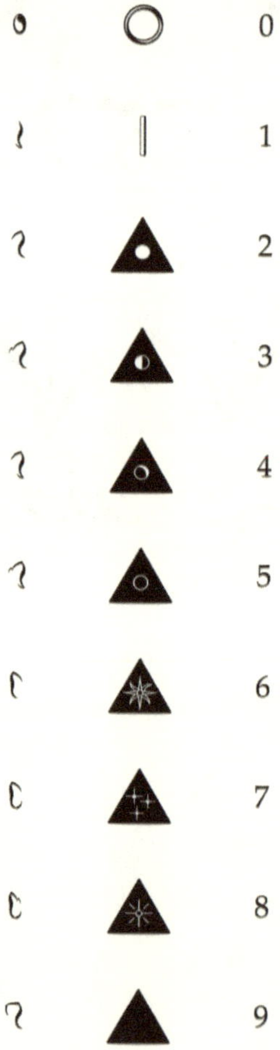

౦	◯	0
౧	∣	1
౨	▲	2
౩	▲	3
౪	▲	4
౫	▲	5
౬	▲	6
౭	▲	7
౮	▲	8
౯	▲	9

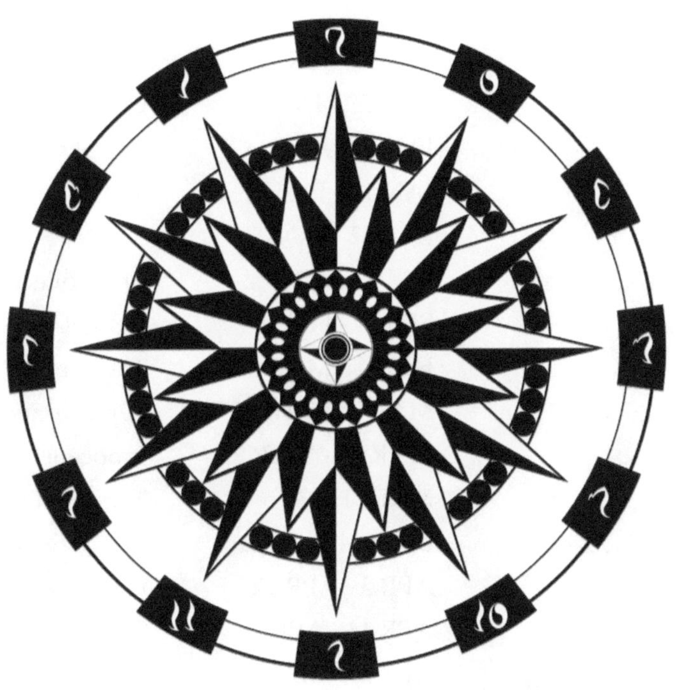

COMPASS	
north	9
eastnorth	0
northeast	7
east	5
southeast	3
eastsouth	10
south	2
westsouth	11
southwest	4
west	6
northwest	8
westnorth	1

		The *Nod* Calendar
	DECEMBER 22	Day One
	DEC 23 - JAN 1	Completion
	JAN 2 - JAN 11	The Sky
	JAN 12 - JAN 21	The Earth
	JAN 22 - JAN 31	Rest
	FEB 1 - FEB 10	The Collective
	FEB 11 - FEB 20	Retreat
	FEB 21 - MAR 2	The Garden
	MAR 3 - MAR 12	Perseverance
	MAR 13 - MAR 22	Innocence
	MARCH 23	Trysting Day
	MAR 24 - APR 2	The Stewpot
	APR 3 - APR 12	Disruption
	APR 13 - APR 22	Stand Still
	APR 23 - MAY 2	The Guardian
	MAY 3 - MAY 12	Repair
	MAY 13 - MAY 22	Unity
	MAY 23	Freshing Day
	MAY 24 - JUN 2	The Mystery
	JUN 3 - JUN 12	Gentleness
	JUN 13 - JUN 22	Courage
	JUNE 23	Lazy Day
	JUN 24 - JUL 3	Joy
	JUL 4 - JUL 13	Sorrow
	JUL 14 - JUL 23	Return
	JUL 24 - AUG 2	Strength
	AUG 3 - AUG 12	Folly
	AUG 13 - AUG 22	The Simple
	AUG 23 - SEP 1	Building

ᒫᖑᒣᒨᖑᑎ:	SEP 2 - SEP 11	The Wild
ᖑᒣᒾᖺᖐᑫᖐᖐᑫᒾ	SEP 12 - SEP 21	Relations
ᒬᒲ ᖌᑌᒣ	SEPTEMBER 22	Berry Day
ᖐᖌᒲᒧ,	SEP 23 - OCT 2	Trust
ᒾᒲᖐ	OCT 3 - OCT 12	The Partner
ᖑᖌᒾᒬᒾ. ᖌᒾᖐᒾᖑᒣᖐ.	OCT 13 - OCT 22	Decisive Action
ᒫᖐᑎᖷ.ᖐᒪᑌᖐ	OCT 23 - NOV 1	Modesty
ᒾᒪᖐ	NOV 2 - NOV 11	Seeking
ᖑ.ᖺᒪᖐᒾ⋮	NOV 12 - NOV 21	Generosity
ᖑ∴ᖺᖑ.	NOV 22 - DEC 1	Mercy
ᖑᖑᖺᖺᒾᖑᖌᒾ⋮	DEC 2- DEC 11	Self-Reliance
꞉ᒪᖑᒲᒲᒾ⋮	DEC 12 - DEC 21	Waiting
ᖺ꞉ᖷᖑᒪᖷᑎ:	LEAP DAY	The Kicker

The dvarsh count moons, but their calendar includes neither weeks nor months. Instead, they divide the year into thirty-six ten-day periods and five holidays. A leap day, *The Kicker*, is added to the end of every fourth year.

Day One, the first day of the dvarsh year, corresponds to December 22 in the Gregorian calendar. Curiously, their leap year coincides with ours as much as the misalignment of start dates allows. The fact that the dvarsh add their leap day at the end also means this table is off much of each leap year. Most of the time, most years, the relationship is stable.

Day One 16,786 corresponds to December 22, 1999 CE in the human West. Called the *Nod* calendar because periods of the year link to auspices of *Nod's Way*, the sequence does not follow the order of the book.

Numeracy

	Pivot	**Power**	**Challenge**
Bar	use	action	concentration
Ring	method	reception	diffusion
0	renewal	rebirth	repetition
1	singularity	focus	obsession
2	encounter	discovery	ambivalence
3	balance	preparation	indifference
4	stability	foundation	stagnation
5	change	advance	humility
6	respite	rest	exhaustion
7	creativity	magic	deceit
8	resource	diversity	excess
9	fulfillment	reward	debt
Face	movement	mastery	incapacity
Hand	release	solace	loss

Before Counting

Before counting, there is turning, there is rising and there is falling.

Before counting fills everything. Everywhere is filled.

Bar is everything that fills. Ring is everywhere that is filled.

Ring turns and rises and falls. Bar does the same.

Bar turns on use. Bar rises to action but falls at the challenge of concentration.

Ring turns on method. Ring rises to reception but falls at the challenge of diffusion.

Ring and bar nest in the shape of being, a nest of absence. The absence, 0, spawns all counts.

0 turns on renewal. 0 rises to rebirth but falls at the challenge of repetition.

From 0 separates 1.

1 turns on singularity. 1 rises to focus but falls at the challenge of obsession.

Ring and bar, 1 contains 2.

2 turns on encounter. 2 rises to discovery but falls at the challenge of ambivalence.

1 seeing 2 sings 3.

3 turns on balance. 3 rises to preparation but falls at the challenge of indifference.

If not right then left, 3 finds 4.

4 turns on stability. 4 rises to foundation but falls at the challenge of stagnation.

The touch of 4 makes 5.

5 turns on change. 5 rises to advance but falls at the challenge of humility.

Beyond 5 appears 6.

6 turns on respite. 6 rises to rest but falls at the challenge of exhaustion.

When 6 wakes there are 7.

7 turns on creativity. 7 rises to magic but falls at the challenge of deceit.

7 weaves the cloth of 8.

8 turns on resource. 8 rises to diversity but falls at the challenge of excess.

8 builds a road to 9.

9 turns on fulfillment. 9 rises to reward but falls at the challenge of debt.

Beyond 9 wears a mask.

The mask turns on movement. The mask rises to mastery but falls at the challenge of incapacity.

There is or is not a hand.

The hand turns on release. The hand rises to solace but falls at the challenge of loss.

ᑐᕆᗱᐤᒍᕆᗱᐧᐸᗱᐧ

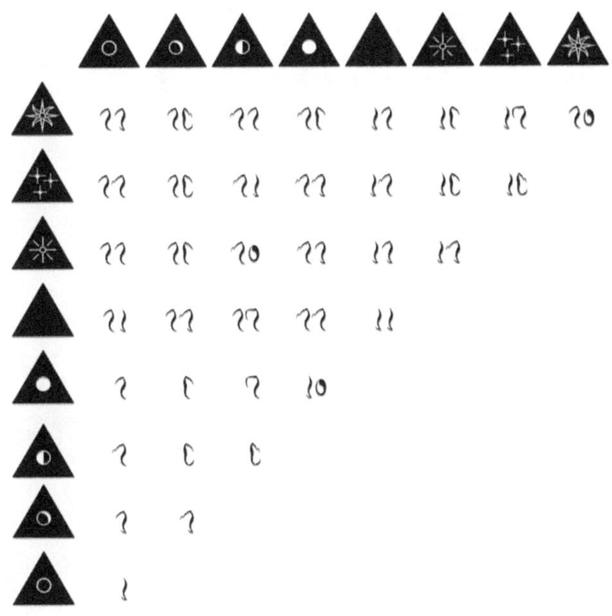

Combinations

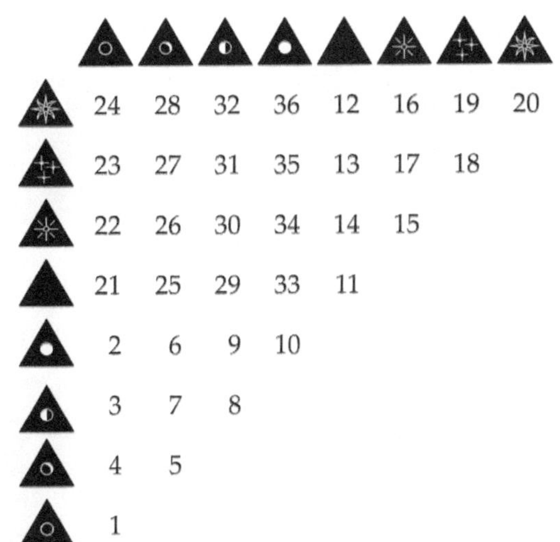

24	28	32	36	12	16	19	20
23	27	31	35	13	17	18	
22	26	30	34	14	15		
21	25	29	33	11			
2	6	9	10				
3	7	8					
4	5						
1							